VERY BORING ALLIGATOR

Henry Holt and Company, LLC
Publishers since 1866
115 West 18th Street
New York, New York 10011

Henry Holt is a registered trademark of
Henry Holt and Company, LLC

Published in Canada by Fitzhenry & Whiteside Ltd.,
195 Allstate Parkway, Markham, Ontario L3R 4T8.

Library of Congress Cataloging-in-Publication Data
Gralley, Jean.
Very boring alligator / by Jean Gralley.
Summary: Simple rhymes describe what happens when
an alligator comes to play and won't go away.
[1. Alligators—Fiction. 2. Stories in rhyme.] I. Title.
PZ8.3.G7297Ve 20001 [E]—dc21 00-44855

ISBN 0-8050-6328-5
First Edition—2001
Printed in the United States of America on acid-free paper. ∞

10 9 8 7 6 5 4 3 2 1

The artist used gouache and ink on watercolor paper
to create the illustrations for this book.

VERY BORING ALLIGATOR

BY  Jean Gralley

Henry Holt and Company
New York

Very Boring Alligator
came one day to play,
but he stay-stay-stayed,
and **HE WOULDN'T GO AWAY.**

I huffed and I sighed.

I made heebie-jeebie eyes.

But that Boring Alligator,

he just **WOULDN'T GO AWAY.**

I said, "Pretty please." (He wouldn't go away.)
I said it on my knees. (He wouldn't go away.)
I said, "You'd better hurry 'cause your
mother's gonna worry!"

But that Gator didn't get it,
AND HE WOULDN'T GO AWAY.

I lurched. I moaned. I gurgled and groaned.
I looked very scary, but he wouldn't go away.
(Grr-grr! Hee-hee! I think you better flee!)

But he stay-stay-stayed, not afrai-frai-fraid.
That Gator didn't GET it,
and he **WOULDN'T GO AWAY**.

All I really wanted
was to slouch upon my couch.
But Gator made me grumpy, oh,
that Gator made me grouch.
When he started **ROMPIN'-STOMPIN'**—
ROMPIN'-STOMPIN' with that tail—

I telephoned the **GATOR COPS** to haul his tail to jail!

They came with sirens wailin'
and their gator poles a-flailin',
they were hootin' and a-railin':
it's a Gator Raider **RAID!**

But when they got
into the house they said . . .

"What a **LOVELY** couch!"

AND WOULD NOT GO AWAY!

They were laughin'
and a-pushin'
and a-jumpin'
on the cushion.
My head
began to pop!
I knew
this had to . . .

Now

Gator comes to play
only when I say,
and at the end of play I say, "Please go away."

And Gator goes away, right away.

'Cause I'm the Boss of Play
every day!